A GHOST STORY

with

JOHN PRIDEAUX OF STOWFORD

(1505 – 1568)

By

A A PRIDEAUX

www.paganuspublishing.co.uk

First Published in 2014

Paganus Publishing

Ruthin

Wales

I am dedicating this book to my family

Story Description

A Ghost Story is exactly what you think it will be. A ghost story. The difference with this one is that it is about a real person, an ancestor of the author.

A A Prideaux has written about each of her Prideaux ancestors from 1040. She has traced every one of them and discovered where and how they lived. A A Prideaux has travelled miles in this search. She has old books, family documents and stories which help in the search and conclusions. These stories bring the Prideauxs to life, giving them personalities and allowing us to know them.

A Ghost Story is one of the fictionalised stories which draw on the known facts. This John Prideaux (1505-1568) story takes us to Dartmoor for a strange ghost story. One day, following an accident he meets the strange Matthew Prowse. This encounter involves him and his friends in a momentous event.
More information can be found on her website. www.aaprideaux.com

You will enjoy the story most, if you read the facts and figures afterwards.

Contents

A Ghost Story

John Prideaux bent down in front of the fire and stabbed at it vigorously with a beautiful brass and iron poker. After a few moments, he was rewarded with yellow and orange flames crackling towards the chimney so he threw several more logs upon the fire. The cheerful blaze finally sent heat and light into the room.

"That's much better, now we can all be a little warmer at last," said Ann Prideaux, relaxing visibly.

The Prideauxs were hosting a dinner party for their friends and family which involved a meal of several courses and expensive brandy and wine. It was their turn this Tuesday. The group took turns each week to entertain on this otherwise uneventful evening.

The dining room had become colder as the meal progressed. When Ann instructed her servants to bring life back into the fire, the obedient Arthur had tried in vain to please his mistress and only succeeded in making the room smokier and darker.

Everyone was pleased when the meal finished and Ann asked the guests to move en masse into the drawing room. She knew that the fire in this room would warm them quickly, without the danger of being suffocated. It is very upsetting to see your guests unable to appreciate the good food put in front of them because they were quietly pulling cloaks and furs about their arms against the cold.

"I apologise for the coldness of the dining room," said Ann to her guests.

"Ann, you are not to worry. The weather at the moment is beyond understanding. I am positive that the winters are getting colder each year. We seem to have more snow now than when I was a boy."

Thomas Rogers lived further along the Kings Highway and was a very good friend to the Prideaux family.

"I agree. The snow was falling quite quickly when we arrived. I am glad we do not need to go home in the carriage tonight," said his wife Joan.

"Are we still hunting tomorrow John, if this weather continues?" Thomas did not like to miss any days hunting.

"We can always go shooting if the horses are not able to get onto the moor," answered John.

Another cousin of John's was a guest that night. He was a regular visitor and confidante of the Prideaux family and the other guests. Parson William Hele was one of the Flete Heles and also had a blood connection to the Heles at Prideaux near St Blazey. John Prideaux and his ancestors were bred there too.

The servants poured more drinks for the guests as Adam Williams walked over to the wooden screens and partly opened them.

"Adam! Shut those screens! Goodness man, we have only just got ourselves warm, I thought I would catch my death of cold tonight!" Robert Fox spoke loudly, but then had the decency to look embarrassed as he realized his hosts were still actually in the room and could hear him. The Prideauxs chose to ignore their cousin and John went over to join Adam at the window.

Adam Williams was married to Alice Prideaux, yet another cousin of John's. The Prideauxs were well connected in the South West and had married into most large and influential families living there. Adam lived at Stowford Manor and was responsible for acres of land which bordered the River Erme and stretched from the Highway to Dartmoor. Alice was the daughter of Thomas Prideaux, a landowner and respected churchwarden at Ashburton. Their children Thomas and Katherine were their pride and joy. Thomas had been admitted to the Inner Temple when he was only 24 and currently had aims to enter Parliament. Katherine was married to a wealthy and suitable gentleman.

It was Alice who had ensured that John Prideaux got the tenancy of this large house and lands from her husband. These lands led directly to the hunting grounds on Dartmoor and bordered land owned by the King.

It was a bonus that all the families got on so well with each other.

"The snow is coming down thick and fast. It is lying too. I expect we shall have drifts by the morning." John said.

"I have to congratulate you on your garden. The moon on the snow makes the place look like a painting! What a pity we cannot capture the scene," said Adam.

The garden was covered in white. Snow hung around the sundial and gave the statues snow hats. The tree branches and clipped box hedges wore snowy cloaks.

"I love the snow," said Ann Prideaux. "I shall walk onto the moors tomorrow if I cannot ride."

John looked across at his wife, proud of her bravery and determination.

"Will you take Johnny and William?" he asked.

"Of course!"

Ann was very proud of her sons. They were the only children they had managed to produce. John knew that Ann was severely disappointed that no girls would be born to them, but the doctor had been quite emphatic after their last child.

"Another pregnancy will likely kill your wife, John. No more children I am afraid."

John took the news well. Some of his contemporaries had taken mistresses at similar news, but so far John had not felt the need.

They closed the wooden screens on the lovely scene and came back into the room.

"Why don't we have dinner with you next week Parson?" This was a long running joke among the group of friends. Although everyone took turns to serve dinner, Hele never did. The others had decided that he was too mean to entertain them and they let no opportunity pass without mentioning it.

Parson Hele was a big man and took no offence.

"Perhaps one day soon," he said.

"Tell us a story. John!" asked Sybil.

John Prideaux was famous for his stories.

"What kind of a story?" he asked his friends.

"A murder story."

"A love story."

"A love story? After dinner on a snowy night with people lost on the moor as we speak? Don't be a stupid woman," Robert shouted at his romantic wife.

The others knew, however, that the only romance his little wife experienced came from this type of romantic storytelling or from books. Her boorish husband covered his romance with a thick layer of infidelity.

She was an unhappy woman.

Suddenly a small voice disturbed the general chatter of the party. It was young Johnny Prideaux who stood in front of the fire, rubbing his eyes.

"Now, Johnny what is the meaning of this?" John senior tried to sound cross, but found it impossible with his boys. Everyone knew that Johnny and his father were particularly close.

"I could not sleep father. I looked out of the window and saw the snow and thought that I should go for a walk on the moor with mother."

"We cannot go now John," said Ann. "We have guests and it is nighttime."

"Father used to travel the moor at night, didn't you father?"

"Yes I did," answered John. He picked up his six year old son and sat him next to Joan on the seat nearest to the fire. Joan put her arms and a fur around the boy and handed him some of her wine and a sweet pastry. Johnny snuggled up to his Aunt Joan happily. Now there was a jolly good chance that he would not be sent back to bed.

"I know what tale I shall tell you all. It is a mystery story and even I do not know how the story ends."

"Well that will be no good. Are we to guess the ending?" asked Thomas.

"Perhaps you could just draw your own conclusions," John answered.

Everyone made themselves comfortable around the fireplace and John sat in his chair in the circle.

Small tables were placed in the middle of the group and housed drinks and food. Little John snuggled closer to Aunt Joan and wisely kept quiet.

"The story I have to tell you is a mystery as I have said. However it is also a true story. I know that because it happened to me."

The audience fell silent and John began.

"My story begins two years ago in 1545. It was a winter's night, very much like this one. The snow was falling heavily and the night quiet and subdued. As the large flakes fell to earth, all the sound from the place vanished. The animals, apart from a hungry fox, had retired into the trees or burrows early in the storm. They were waiting until the daylight brought some respite and they could safely scurry and fly out looking for food. As the evening wore on, the wind died down but the snow kept on falling.

The only reason I was out on this winter's night was to help a friend of mine. He had asked me to meet him as a matter of life and death. I set off at five in the afternoon, complete with lamp and walking stick. I wrapped myself in a heavy wool cloak, a scarf and hat. I was a lonely figure as I trudged from Stowford towards Dartmoor.

"Don't go out in this weather sir," the housekeeper had said to me. "You could come to harm and none of us would know until it was too late. Your wife would not be pleased if I reported that I had let you out on a night like this."

"Not to worry about me Mrs. Tamm. I shall be back before midnight. Keep the fires burning for me and leave me some food out and I shall be happy."

Ann was away at her parents with the boys and so I had no other explanations to make.

I went out into the snow, turning back to look at my house once or twice. I noticed the lights in the window for a little while, but I was surprised just how quickly I lost sight of the house as the snow fell. I kept my mind on the journey in hand and continued head down, following my feet along the track I knew by heart, even though it was covered in deep snow.

You will all know that, when it is snowing very heavily and although the snow is fresh and white, the effect is of complete and utter darkness. Those narrow lanes and the high hedges made me feel as though I was walking along a tunnel to heaven or to hell. I'm not sure which. I found it lonely and other worldly that evening and began to imagine all kinds of strange things.

I found my mind running to the stories I had heard over the years about beasts and phantoms and witches. As I wiped the snow from my face, I stopped to look and listen. There was nothing, no sound, no movement around me and I started to lose my bearings.

I was becoming a little anxious and thought about what would happen if I died of cold and could not be found until the spring. I could not see myself, so how would anyone see me?

"John you are a silly person." I told myself.

I was going to meet my friend Matthew. You may ask what sort of a friend wants you to meet him on Dartmoor, late at night in the middle of a snow storm? Well he was quite a good one actually.

I met Matthew Prowse while out riding one summer day on Ugborough Moor. It was in the 30's. I was on my own, except for my hounds and my horse and was just enjoying the day. Suddenly, my horse spooked at a bird flying from the bracken, I was thrown and hit the ground with some force. I must have been knocked out for a time, because when I opened my eyes a strange man was looking at me in a concerned way.

"Are you alright sir?" he asked.

"Well yes I think so. What happened?"

"You were thrown from your horse and hit your head."

"Oh. Is my horse alright? Where are my hounds?"

"Don't worry, they are all fine." The man seemed amused at my questions.

I sat up and took stock of the situation. My animals may be fine, but I felt very queasy. The man helped me to my feet and upon seeing how wobbly I was, insisted that I accompanied him to his house. I did not feel like arguing and followed him to his black carriage which stood nearby. I cannot remember much about the journey, but very soon we were arriving at the front door of a large stone property which had ivy growing up the front of the house, almost covering the windows.

Inside the house it was dark, even though the sun shone brightly on this August day. We had left a bright moor, almost scorched from the long drought we had been experiencing. But standing in the hallway, I felt cold and shivery. Perhaps it was the shock setting in.

Matthew Prowse, for we had now been introduced, insisted I go into the library, where a large fire had been lit. I sat in front of it and accepted gratefully the sustenance he offered.

It seems that Matthew had lived here on his own, with only a few servants, ever since his wife died in childbirth five years prior. He had not felt the need to find another wife, preferring his own company and that of his two hounds.

"Are you not lonely here?" I asked him.

"No, I have my faith and know that the Lord will assist me to carry out whatever purpose he has for me," was the strange reply.

Now, I was as well aware then as I am today, that to talk of one's religious beliefs in front of a stranger is a very dangerous thing to do. So I kept my peace and asked no more.

I spent the next hour or two admiring the books in his library and the fine furniture and tapestries in his house. We talked about many things and found that we got on famously. I wondered how much religion did feature in his life as I noticed an altar in the corner of the library with candles, seemingly constantly lit. There was a Latin Bible which Matthew saw me examining, but he said nothing, merely smiled.

After supper, I was loaded onto the carriage and my horse tied to the back. My hounds were allowed to travel in the carriage with me. The coachman drove me home as Matthew waved to me from his driveway. I had accepted an invitation to supper the following evening, before leaving.

I did join him for supper the next evening and for several evenings after that. Matthew never came to my house nor accompanied me anywhere else. I enjoyed his company and we laughed and had great fun together. I was not married then and I often found the time hanging heavy unless I spent it with Matthew. Both my parents were dead and my brother Hugh busy with his inheritance at Luson. Henry and Thomas my other two brothers also found that their lands kept them busy. I have to admit that until I met Matthew, I was also constantly busy with my own properties. Suddenly these responsibilities were taking a back seat.

We spent time riding, hunting and playing cards. We also discussed religion and his upset at the reforms of King Henry and his marriage to 'that harlot'. I soon realized he was not a fan of hers.

"It is not right that so many good people are losing their lives in such terrible ways. I personally find the King's unpredictable explosions quite unnerving. I have been present for a few of them and so have removed myself here, far away from his ravings and his presence."

I learnt that Matthew had made his feelings known to the King and suffered his temper and his disapproval. Matthew had been able to leave the Court with little fuss even though other influences at court had made him nervous. He felt that some wanted to be rid of him permanently. I liked the man and did not want anything to happen to him.

Perhaps if I am honest, I was also impressed with the names he mentioned. The fact that our family had long been involved in the same circles as Matthew made the stories so very interesting.

I did not see him quite as much once I married and he was often busy, in London, he said.

Once he told me something that has stayed with me to this very day.

"There are really more things in heaven and earth that are not understood. The King has started to make people believe that all relics and rituals are dangerous and evil and that they don't work. There are also many who know that this is not true and will do whatever is necessary to preserve the good old ways. I would like to show you how we can have an amazing influence on our own life if only we knew what to do."

I listened to him and kept an open mind. For it has to be said, my grandfather had similar beliefs. Grandfather told me that none of our family needs to rely on others for our salvation. It rests completely with us.

Matthew continued, "I have some books here in my library and some relics hidden well away that will explain how this can be done. On no account must you mention this to anyone else John. For if you do I may not be able to stay here and I must ask you to promise me something."

"I will if I can Matthew."

"Thank you John. Soon Christmas will be here and I must travel to London in disguise. There, I shall meet a friend and will return home in the New Year. I must ask you to meet me here on the 28th January no matter what else is occurring in your life. No matter what else!" He emphasized the point firstly, by repetition and secondly, by leaning into my face.

"Why? What is going to happen on that night?" I was becoming a little worried by my friend's demeanor.

"You only need to know that the date is important. I should also tell you that it might not be next January."

I promised him that I would and also said that I would make sure that I returned each and every 28th January until I saw him again.

"Don't make rash promises you have no intention of keeping," Matthew answered.

"I just promised you, did I not? Now are you going to let me see these relics? I would be very much interested in them."

Matthew looked at me and I could see that he was wondering whether or not to let me in on his secret. I was interested, but if honest I was also more than a little skeptical about the things he told me. I would be a fool not to admit that relics were around the country and I had heard tales of their magical properties. There were tales of eternal life, flying, travelling to other worlds in addition to the more mundane tales of wart curing and love potions.

"Follow me," he said eventually and got up from his chair. I followed him out of the room and across the hall to the library. He walked over to a bookcase which heaved with books, manuscripts and old papers. I had leafed through these documents on many occasions during my visits to him and found nothing more exotic than history books, personal papers and some court documents.

He looked at me again and said,

"You promise never to talk about what you are about to see?" I gave him my promise and thus appeased, he hit a small gargoyle on the central pillar and a door opened in the shelves. I stood amazed for a moment but soon followed my friend into the darkness.

Matthew carried a torch and I could see what lay in the small space beyond the library shelves. I was shocked and saddened and overcome with an overwhelming emotional release and I cried.

"You see why I made you promise?" he asked.

"Yes," was all I could answer.

"What was it? What did you see?" asked my audience.

"I made a promise and I intend to keep it." John told them.

"You can't do that!" said Robert.

"If I may be allowed to continue with my tale?"

John was met with nods from everyone. He was happy to see that he had their complete and utter attention. More wood was put on the fire, more food and drink handed around and John continued.

"As soon as I saw the contents of the room, I understood why Matthew was so protective and why others would kill him in order to possess the items.

"Matthew, how long have you known about these?"

"I learnt about them at Oxford. I met academics who knew and I eventually was entrusted with some of the things when our great and glorious King fell for this whore. They were insisting that all relics must be destroyed."

"Because these things prove the existence of other worlds and our ability to reach them?"

"Exactly."

"May I touch?"

Upon receiving a positive answer, I entered the room and touched and held the items. It felt as though I had come home.

I departed my friend's house that night feeling like a different person. I waved goodbye to him and repeated my promise to return on the 28th of the following month.

That brings me back to the night I was telling you about. The journey to Matthew's house took over four hours by the time I made my way through the high drifts. Immediately I noticed that there were very few signs of life at the house. Well, none in fact. There were no lamps at the window and no evidence of smoke from the chimneys. Although to be honest I would have had difficulty seeing that in the snow. But there is always a smell of smoke is there not? There was no smell, but I knocked at the door nevertheless. There was no answer, so I pulled the huge knocker further away from the door and dropped it heavily against the oak. The noise made me jump, never mind anyone in the house and I waited for a time. There was still no answer. So I made the decision to open the door.

I did not expect it to be locked. Matthew never had his door locked as the servants were always present. The door opened quite easily and I made my way inside. The hall was deserted and felt freezing cold. I had the same feeling any normal person has when they enter a house without invitation, one of guilt. It is as if the spirit of the house is giving all of the attention to you as an uninvited guest.

I shivered involuntarily and made my way to the kitchen in the hope of finding a lamp and fire of some sort.

The kitchen was almost as cold as the rest of the house, but I saw that a fire had been lit and although it now only held smouldering logs, there was hope there. I rattled away with a poker after adding some more kindling and dry straw. The fire began to show more life and I used the flame to light a lamp. I filled up a kettle with water and put this onto a hook which hung over the flames. I intended to fill a warming bottle and if I was lucky enough to find some wine, would warm that too.

I looked around the room and saw that everything appeared to be in order. But there was not the fresh food about I had been used to seeing during my visits to Matthew. It was very odd. I soon had to accept that Matthew was not at home and perhaps there was a servant only coming rarely to check the place. I rummaged around and found some biscuits and ate a few. The wine helped warm my body which was almost frozen solid. My mind must have been frozen too as I was beginning to think more logically as I warmed up.

This was odd. Where was my friend and why had he not returned? Where were the servants?

I put more logs on the fire and took the lamp with me as I went to explore the rest of the house. I started with the kitchen and the rooms off that. All the windows were closed firmly, but the back door was unlocked. I opened it and saw Matthew's two large hounds standing at the back door. They looked thin and pitiful and jumped at me wagging their tails in recognition. Being a dog lover, my heart went out to these poor beasts that seemed to have had to fend for themselves for a considerable time. I brought them in to the warm kitchen and opened the biscuit box and shared out the remains between the dogs. They helped me in the pantry as we found some salted beef which they ate hungrily. I decided there and then to take them home with me.

They walked with me around the house and I felt much braver being accompanied by these two huge dogs sniffing ahead of me. The result of the search proved only that no one was living here and had not for some time. Matthew's bedchamber was cold and dusty and I still found it a little creepy with only the lamplight casting shadows ahead of me and the wind howling against the windows. I was sure that the feeling of a haunted house would be similar to this.

As I stood at the top of the stairs, now having explored everywhere, I thought of the little room in the library which Matthew had shown me on my last visit. I thought that I should check that.

I called the dogs and went to the library. I had a sudden desire to light a second lamp in case I lost the light from the first one. I did not think that I could stand for that to happen. Thus prepared I went to the shelves and touched the same gargoyle I had seen Matthew touch but nothing happened. I tried again and still nothing. I looked along the shelves in case there was another gargoyle I had missed, but there wasn't.

I went over to Matthew's desk and decided to have a look in the drawers. There I found a document addressed to 'My friend John Prideaux.' I opened it and read.

John,

If you are reading this, it is January 28th and I am not here. Don't give up on me and return every 28th January until you find me again.

I am putting my faith in you.

Matthew

I reread it and found nothing that could be construed as a hidden secret message. So, I went back to the kitchen and stoked up the fire again. I don't really know why I did this, but had thoughts about other travelers who may need warmth. I blew out the lamps and went out of the back door with the dogs following closely.

Looking back over my shoulder, I thought I saw a light upstairs, but it must have been a trick of my eyes because it was not there now.

I pulled my cloak tighter about me and trudged back to my own house. When I came back in through my own front door over three hours later, I was greeted with a warm feeling.   I saw the fires and lamps lit and there was a wonderful smell of hot food. What a difference to the house I had visited so recently.

My own hounds met me ecstatically and greeted Matthew's hounds with equal enthusiasm. We all trouped into the kitchen and found soup and pasties warming on the iron plate over the fire. A meal has never been more welcome before or since."

John Prideaux stopped speaking and looked at his audience who had not uttered a word. The spell was broken and Alice Williams said,

"So what happened next?"

"I said it was a mystery, I have never found out what happened to this day."

"You cannot leave us with a story half told John! That is not fair!"

"Well, perhaps if you ask me some questions we can work out what happened that night," said John.

"Did you go back to the house again?" asked Adam.

"I did and each year the house has become colder and felt more haunted. A servant goes there and cleans up and lights fires when necessary, he says that his master intends to return one day. He has been paid to work there and work there he will."

"Who pays him then?" persisted Adam.

"Some lawyer, I believe. These lawyers keep the place maintained, but will say nothing about their client's whereabouts or intentions."

"What happened to the dogs?" asked Joan, ever the animal lover.

"We still have them. Bat and Spangle live with us here in the house and we have given the pups from them and my own dogs to some of you," said Ann.

"We have had two ourselves. I hadn't realized where they came from," said Adam.

"As long as they have a happy life. I was worried about them having nothing to eat and being cold and lonely out there in the snow," Joan said timidly.

Her husband Thomas raised his eyes to the heavens in despair.

"Ann just told you that they are here in this house and they have puppies and everything!"

"Oh! I thought she meant just John's own dogs!"

The gathering giggled a little and then continued with their questions.

"So can you tell us know what you saw in the little room?"

"No."

"I have never heard of you going about with this Matthew chap, when did that happen?" asked Thomas.

"We do not live in each other's pockets, Thomas. We all have friends the others do not know about," said Parson Hele.

Alice suddenly said, "Forgive me, but is it not the 28th January tonight?"

Everyone turned to look at her, and began talking all at once.

"So it is!"

"There is nothing for it, we must go out tonight."

"In this snow?"

"John has travelled there before in the snow. Come on John. Show us the way!"

If this outcome had been John's intention, then it was going accordingly to plan. Perhaps he was tired of travelling to the house in the woods on his own and wanted some help. As it was, only half an hour had passed before the men were well wrapped up and had collected lamps and food and wine. They carried sticks and had several hounds spinning about their heels, excited about the late night adventure.

The women waved them off at the door and immediately settled themselves by the fire talking of the silliness of men, while all quietly wishing they could go too.

"The men are so brave," said Joan.

"Not really, they have all the excitement, never us," answered Ann.

The women set about taking Johnny upstairs, as he had fallen fast asleep in Joan's arms.

"It's a pity he won't have a sister Ann," said Joan without thinking.

Ann patted her stomach. "I am with child now Joan, But John does not know, so don't tell him."

"I thought the doctor told you that would be too dangerous?" asked Alice in horror.

"I am sure it will be fine. I feel so well."

The other ladies looked at each other, they knew that the doctor's warning had been serious and were worried for their friend.

The men set off in the thick snow, tramping the virgin whiteness with their leather boots and carrying heavy hazel sticks. Their outward appearances changed as the snow covered their clothing.

John Prideaux looked at his friends, thinking how different this trip was to his other adventures. No lonely trudge through the snow now. Everyone laughed and joked and pushed each other about. They were not acting like the gentleman of Stowford and Ermington, more like schoolboys on a mystery tour.

"We should be very thankful that we do not have to cross the river. Now that would be a battle," said Adam.

The four men followed John along the Harford road and after an hour the talking and joking subsided. They were using all of their energy just lifting their legs high out of the snow. They saw no one else on their travels except an old fox which had braved the storm to look for food.

"I have just had a thought," said Robert Fox after two hours of trudging.

"We should drink to that!" Adam quipped. Adam, although 57 years old, was as fit as any man there and had a razor sharp mind.

"Oh ha-ha! But I am being serious, I have never seen a house where you described and my father has never mentioned one."

The others began murmuring their agreement.

John carried on walking, but for the first time in the ten years he had known Matthew, considered the fact that he had never heard of a house there before either.

They walked past Harford Church, where they spent part of their Sundays and attended weddings and christenings. The few cottages on the lane were well shuttered and closed to the snowy outside world they were walking through.

Parson Hele said, "My little church looks so lonely tonight."

"Don't worry Parson, its only asleep," said John comfortingly.

They passed the parsonage, also in darkness, save for one lamp at a downstairs window and within a hundred steps, were on the moor. They struggled as they trudged slowly through the deepening snow. The blizzarding storm ensured they kept their heads well down and it would have been easy to forget which way the track headed. The strong wind howled and screamed as it travelled from one sea to another.

"We must be the only fools out on the moor," shouted Adam, for now the noise of the wind was increasing dramatically as they climbed higher. There was almost nothing stopping in its path as it flew across the moor.

"We are not fools!" answered Adam. "We are adventurers!"

He was unable to hear any answer because the snow hit their faces and bodies with such force that it was becoming difficult to stand upright against it.

Eventually they reached a familiar row of ancient standing stones and walked for another half an hour beyond them. It was here that John expected to see the house. He stopped in his tracks.

"It's not there!" he said.

"Perhaps you have taken a wrong turning," said Robert.

"I can't have done, I have made this journey many times. I have walked it and ridden it. I don't understand this." John was truly confused.

"Well, my friend, you need to find the place soon. The weather is not improving and I for one am getting a little tired." said Adam.

John looked around and said to his friends.

"But, I do not understand this. The house should be here, right here!"

"It isn't here though, is it?" said his parson cousin gently. "Follow me back to the church and we can shelter and have a think."

"Why not your house Hele?" asked Adam reasonably.

Parson Hele only said, "We cannot disturb my servants this late. We shall be safe at the church."

"Safe? From what?" asked Robert.

"Come on John. I for one am not happy about being on the moor any longer than I have to be."

By now, the swirls of snow appeared to be going back up to the heavens as fast as they were coming down. It created a spinning tunnel effect and was starting to look menacing, rather than beautiful.

John nodded without speaking, but did turn around and the others followed. There were all now trying to find their previous footsteps before they were obliterated.

It was another hour before he led the men and hounds past the parsonage and through the door of St Petrocs. The door banged shut and Thomas dropped the latch.

"You see, I knew where the church was and this place is just as difficult to find as Matthew's house. Why can I not see the house?"

"Don't worry yourself John. Use your energy on keeping warm and not on thinking about things you can do nothing about."

"I will, William. It's certainly cold enough in here."

"It is cold in here. Your church is bad enough on a Sunday morning, but apparently on a Tuesday night it is even worse," complained Adam. "Why can't we go into your house Parson?"

William Hele said nothing, but the look on his face quelled any further questions.

"At least we are out of that rotten wind and snow for a while," said Robert.

"But when we were moving I felt warmer than I do now. I think I am wet through my cloak." Adam took it off and shook the snow from it. He hung the dark cloak over the back of a pew.

"John, is this a joke? Part of your mystery story? If so I am very impressed that you brought us out here under false pretences. Very clever, but now can we go home?" Robert was becoming annoyed.

"No, it is not a joke! I don't understand what is happening here. It is all a bit mad." John sat on a pew holding his face in his heads as though in desolate prayer.

"We should try and get some heat and light going, before we all catch our deaths," said Thomas.

Robert found a taper in a jar by the altar and used it to begin lighting the candles around the church. The others followed his lead, glad to have their minds taken away from their cold limbs. Soon the place looked much more cheerful as the lanterns sent a glow around the beautiful small church.

"Someone may see what is happening here and walk over," said Robert. "One of your servants Parson?"

"Not likely, not in this weather. I wager that they won't even be able to see the lights at the windows, especially if they have their own screens closed," reasoned Adam.

Robert Fox looked out of the window, cupping his hands around his eyes in order to eliminate the light from inside the church.

"It looks creepy out there now," he observed. "Mark you, its creepy in here too."

The others nodded their heads. There was a collective feeling of waiting for their fate among the group. A grim fate.

The candles and lanterns did not reach the dark corners and even the pulpit had a shadow across it.

"We should stay here for a while until we get warmer and have a better idea of what is going on," said John. Inwardly, he was becoming concerned for his own sanity. He was feeling confused and more than a little stupid.

"Was this Matthew man a ghost do you think?" asked Robert.

"No such thing as ghosts," said Adam. He was becoming concerned about the way the night was going and was trying very hard, not to think about ghosts.

"What is your view on ghosts Parson?" asked Adam, who was still feeling peeved that they were not sitting in the parsonage in front of the fire there. He had no doubt it would be roaring and there would be food and wine.

Parson Hele was quiet for a time, but then beckoned them all to sit. He went over to the altar and opened a chest. Reaching in, he produced wine, beakers and a large cake.

"A cake? William, a cake?" asked Robert.

"Some of my ladies like to give me things," he answered, "and my servants do not want these gifts in the house."

"You mean that witch of a housekeeper you have doesn't allow it," said John. "You should get rid of the woman."

"Or marry her," laughed Adam.

Parson Hele sat down and said, "I have a tale of my own if you want to hear it."

"We might as well listen to your tale," said Adam. "While we wait for the weather to improve."

Everyone agreed and fell silent.

"I am constantly asked why people are rarely allowed at my home and never after dark. Perhaps now would be a good time to let you all know why that is. I have been parson here since 1521, when I took over from Parson John Teake..."

"My God!" exclaimed Robert. "Is it really that long? Well, I hope you last as long as that old boy did, he was quite ancient when he finally went off to meet his employer!"

"Yes, although the problem seems to be, that he never actually left."

"Ah, I see. Is this to be a ghost story to match John's?" asked Adam.

"I don't know whether it matches, but it is a ghost story," answered Parson Hele.

"Oh excellent," said John. He was feeling brighter now.

"My family at Flete thought I should take up a local benefice and was employed soon after Parson Teake was buried. You were instrumental in that Adam. Teake had taken most of the services, in spite of his great age until he was too ill to continue. I assisted with the duties until he took his last breath and took over completely after that. I took his funeral service and have never had a day off since. It has to be said however, that Teake was not pleased with me. It was not so much me, as anyone taking over from him. St Petrocs was his and he told me that he never wanted to leave. The church had been known as St George the Martyr, but the tinners didn't want that and have always referred to it as St Petrocs. He wanted to call it St George, but I have always said St Petrocs."

"Partly my fault," said Adam. "Thought I could hide our church and keep the workers happy at the same time. Teake always was a fool."

"I like St Petroc," said John.

Parson Hele smiled in respect to their mutual Cornish roots and continued.

"Even when he was quite ill, he did not appreciate the help I gave him, instead choosing to criticise. I was not permitted to stay at the Parsonage, but boarded instead at Lukesland. Even in his last days I would arrive at the church to find him taking the services, at the wrong times. He would be at the pulpit, half dressed and with straggled hair, preaching that we were all doomed to hell."

"I remember that," said Adam. "We used to think that you weren't helping him much as it appeared that he had to preach even though he was so ill. Then we soon realized that his erratic behavior was due to his failing mind and after he died, we forgot about it."

"Well it seems that he didn't forget about it. His last words to me were. 'You bastard. You are killing me so you can steal my home and my church! I won't ever leave!'

And he didn't. After he was buried, I moved to the Parsonage and took his old rooms changing little save for adding my possessions. That first night I was woken by him standing at the bottom of my bed, staring at me in the most alarming way. I told him to leave and he did. Sadly, he continued to return night after night. Soon there came talk of lights in the church during the early hours. I went to check and saw my predecessor standing at the pulpit, dressed shoddily and preaching his hell fire to the empty pews. He could see me however and he would stare and point his finger in my direction, cursing me all the while."

"Why have you never told us?" asked Robert.

"In case you thought I was mad, but apparently I am not the only mad one in our group! Now we have John. But my visitations have happened almost every night since Teake's death. Teake preaches from the pulpit through the night hours and interspersed with these sermons, will spend time at the Parsonage. He frightens the few servants who will stay. Mrs. Morton is one of those few who will remain with me. But even she will lock herself into her rooms soon after seven, saying that is the only way she feels safe. I can have no guests when there is a white haired spirit roaming around the corridors, shouting and swearing. I do not know how to get rid of him and am limited to what can be done to a supposed holy man."

"So, is he here tonight? I mean, are we in the presence of ghosts? I thought we were safe in a church," cried Adam.

"You are safe in the church," he answered.

"Tonight got me thinking in a different way after you told your relic story John. I hope I can trust you all, but during my time here I have found relics and texts, which I should have relinquished during these recent troubles. There is also some plate and silver crosses which would be taxable if I had ever told of their existence."

Adam Williams said,

"I am not so sure I should be hearing about this. My position requires that I tell the authorities."

"But you are not going to are you? We want no more interference in our lives here than is necessary." Robert said.

"No, no I am not. I am not interested in our selfish King and his taxations. He gets enough contribution from me for his wars and weddings. Are we allowed to see these relics of yours, as we are not allowed to see the ones belonging to your Matthew friend?"

"Sadly, they are not here in the church. I have them hidden in the cellars at the house. I will show them to you another time. In the daylight, when we shall not be interrupted. I don't think my predecessor approved of these Petroc relics. He kept them well hidden even though he was the person who showed me where they were. I wonder if he regrets doing that. "

"Well I hope he doesn't turn up tonight to give us a stern sermon," noted Robert.

There was a loud knock at the church door.

A knock at a door in normal circumstances means nothing more than a welcome or an unwelcome guest, either was possible.

But, in the middle of the night at a lonely church door on Dartmoor, in a snow storm?

The five nervous men stood like statues.

The knock came again.

"God above! What can this mean?" whispered Adam.

"If it is a ghost or a phantom rector or a monster of any kind, I shall drop dead on the spot," whispered Robert.

John realized that the dogs were not barking or whimpering, but instead were sniffing at the door.

Emboldened by this, he said, "I shall answer the door, you cowards!"

He went over to the door, lifted the latch and his jaw dropped as soon as he saw the owner of the knock.

"Who is it?" hissed Adam.

John opened the door fully and stepping aside, beckoned in the visitor.

"My friends, let me introduce Matthew Prowse!"

Matthew Prowse walked confidently into the church, hand outstretched.

"I am very pleased to meet you all. John, I am honored that you returned to help me as instructed. You are a true friend indeed. But here, I must introduce you all to a companion of mine. Henry, do come in."

A very fat man followed Matthew into the church. He was red bearded and had one of the roundest faces John had ever seen in his life. The man looked confused and asked them all if they were monks.

"I have been plagued by monks recently," he informed them.

"No, we are not monks. We are men on an adventure, which has turned out rather differently than the one we expected." Adam answered. He felt that this man was familiar to him, but could not work out why.

"My day has turned out differently too. Why, earlier this day I was lying in my bed contemplating the sins I have committed in my life and regretting most of them. I hope Edward makes a better job of it than I did," said Henry.

The others looked confused but decided to say nothing. The man did not look very well.

"Come inside sir and warm yourself. Close the door John, the snow is coming in," Adam. He thought that the man looked as though he could drop down dead at any moment.

"Have some cake and wine. You look as though you need it."

"Thank you, you are very kind. I have not been a kind man, but I have been brave."

The friends pulled faces to each other and made room for the man who they considered was probably simple minded.

"Matthew, you have some explaining to do, I think," John said to his old friend.

"All in good time John."
"How is it that I cannot find your house?"

"I don't know what you are talking about John." Matthew smiled broadly. "My house is exactly where I left it."

John took Matthew to one side and said,

"Now look here, I have come back here every 28th January since we spoke last and several times during the year too. The least you can do is offer me some sort of explanation. And who is this man? He seems ill."

"Perhaps he is known to you in some small way John."

John looked at Matthew and began to think that his friend was going peculiar.

William Hele walked over to the visitors and stared into the face of Henry.

"Do I know you sir?" he asked.

"I don't think so. Are you a monk? The monks have been pestering me for a long time. Telling me about hell and such. There is one of them over there!" he said, pointing to the pulpit. "I must apologise to you sir!"

Everyone looked towards the pulpit, but they saw no one.

"Come along Henry, we must make tracks. We need to arrive before dawn," said Matthew.

"What time is it now?" asked Henry.

"It is after four in the morning."

"So, tomorrow already. They will remember the 28th as the end for me. It is over."

Henry got up from his chair and took Adam's hand.

"I thank you again for your kindness sir. I think that one day soon, your son Thomas will meet my daughter Elizabeth. He must tell her the whereabouts of some belongings of mine and give her this ring. She will reward him with an excellent job and other assets. Tell her I am sorry and I love her. I will speak to her when she is older. Remember, I am talking about Elizabeth and not Mary. I cannot speak to Mary, she is scarred and poisoned by her mother's words."

Henry whispered something in the ear of Adam and shook the hands of everyone else present. He had tears in his eyes as he preceded Matthew out of the door.

Suddenly Henry stopped and said to John, "Mr. Prideaux, take my staff and use it well. I am grateful for your help."

John did as he was bid and took the oak and gold staff. It had a royal crest carved into the gold.

"Matthew!" hissed John, aware that he sounded like a cross wife.

"John! Yes, you deserve an explanation of sorts. I know that you have not told anyone of the contents of the room I showed you. They would not believe you anyway and probably not what I am about to tell you. But, here goes. I have a specific job in this world. You remember how we first met?"

"Of course, you found me after I fell from my horse."

"I did. Consider this, if you had died that day and not been knocked out, your children would not have been born nor their children nor their...... You get the point. Descendants of yours will have important tasks to complete and so it was imperative that you lived and had heirs. Dying prematurely would have made this impossible. So, if my specific job were to collect the dead and guide them on their journey, I would no doubt be allowed certain discretions in the few occasions I consider necessary. Perhaps your fall was one of those times."

Matthew stopped and watched his audience. John still seemed confused. The other men assumed it was some sort of personal matter in which they should not interfere; they certainly didn't understand what was being said. Parson Hele was the only one who appeared to understand.

"What about all the things you told me and showed me?"

"All true. But, you will never find the house again in this life. Not in this life," he repeated.

"What about all the things in the library?"

"One day you may see them again." Matthew said mysteriously.

"Why was I supposed to keep coming on the 28th January?"

"Because I knew the date was important and I had to have someone I trusted to open this church for me. This church is a sainted gateway to the next world and I needed to travel through Dartmoor with this man. I took his father through Cadair Idris in Wales, but this Henry had to come to Dartmoor. It's to do with Arthur."

"Arthur Tresidda from Theuborough?" asked Adam.

"No, not that one, a much older man. He has been dead years," answered Matthew, looking amused.

"I don't understand what all this had been about," said Robert.

"No, I don't expect you do Robert. But John, thank you for being my friend and for your kindness to me. Here, take this paper and memorise the prayer written down upon it. It is a special prayer for the Prideaux family and can be read or sung or just remembered. Have Ann say it if she is ever ill or in trouble. Tell your descendants to be kind to others and luck and good fortune will follow, I shall see to that. Goodnight all! I guarantee that we shall all meet again one day!"

On that cheery note he left the church.

"The man is mad!" said Robert.

The wind was still howling against the church walls and the snow beat against its old windows as though it would smash them.

"Let's go home," said John and began to put out the candles.

"Agreed! Who do you think they were really? I don't think anyone will believe us about tonight." Robert was very confused and unhappy.

"I am having a great time!" said Adam. "I don't see how I can beat this at my dinner party next week! Although you were a close second to John with your scary rector story Hele!"

Once the candles and lamps had been extinguished, St Petrocs church regained its lonely spirit.

"Why are churches so grim and frightening?" asked Adam.

"I know, there is nothing welcoming about an empty church," agreed John.

"Especially when it is dark," said Parson Hele.

John made sure his friends were outside on the path before he shut the heavy door. As he was about to latch it, he heard someone talking inside. He opened the door quietly and saw the old rector preaching from the pulpit.

He turned towards John, pointing ominously with his outstretched fingers.

"Death is on its way to your house John Prideaux!"

John slammed the door and turned back to the others.

"Are you quite well John? You look as though you have seen a ghost!" said Adam cheerily.

"I fear we have all seen ghosts tonight," muttered Robert. No one felt the need to answer him and they walked down the path to the gate.

Parson Hele smiled and told his friends that he would return, quietly, to his house and go straight to bed. There had been a lot of excitement tonight.

Taking their leave, the rest of the band began their return journey down to Stowford. The snow had stopped and the wind had quietened down. It was a beautiful night and the men felt their energies rise as they made the trip home. They began to joke around and laugh again.

"I wonder what he meant about Ann?"

"What do you mean?"

"He said, that she should recite the prayer if she ever became ill."

"He meant nothing in particular, I don't think. He just said to give her the prayer."

"Look over there!" said John suddenly.

They all stopped and looked   across the moor. A very bright light with a rainbow aura appeared in the sky. It was as if a bonfire had been lit and fireworks set off.

"What was that?" asked Robert.

"Probably another ghost," said Adam.

It didn't generally take as long to return to Stowford as the other way about, it being downhill. But tonight, the deep snowdrifts meant that every step involved lifting their legs as high as they could in an effort to clear the snow.

It was dawn by the time they arrived back home. They were met by the wives who were anxious to hear their news. The women had slept in turns by the fire and now instructed the waking servants to serve an early breakfast. The women listened in awe and would not have believed the story had not all four men stuck to the same theme.

"What was the prayer John?" asked Ann gently.

John took the papers from his pocket and began to read,

O God, That knowest us to bee set in the midst of so many and great dangers, that for Mans frailenesse we cannot always stand uprightly, guard to us the health of Body and Soul, that all of those things which we suffer for sinne, by thy holy wee passe and overcome through Jesus Christ our Lord

Young John Prideaux listened to all from his hidey hole on the balcony and thought he would never forget this night.

It was a day later when Ann Prideaux ran into her husband's study and said,

"Guess what I have just heard in the town?"

"I cannot imagine." John answered drily.

"The King is dead! He died two days ago and Edward is our new King. What about that!"

John put down his book and looked out of his window at the moor.

"What about that indeed," he answered.

Footnotes

- A staff which once belonged to King Henry VIII was given by the Bishop of Worcester John Prideaux to his son in law upon his death. The Bishop was the grandson of the John Prideaux in this ghost story.
- William Hele was related to the Prideauxs in the manner described in this story.
- The prayer quoted, was handed down through the Prideaux family and repeated by them. Bishop John kept the simple prayer with him throughout his extraordinary life. The prayer and the staff features in The Bishop and the Witch, by A A Prideaux.
- Ann Prideaux died young, possibly during pregnancy or childbirth. There were only two sons born to the marriage.
- William Hele was the parson at St Petrocs church from 1521
- John Teake was the parson for many years until 1521. The previous rector John Forde, joined St Petrocs in 1431 and the years in between were shared between the two. I am not exactly sure when Forde left and Teake began.

- Most documents refer to the church at Harford as St Petrocs. There is however Document 422 at Devon CRO dated 20/03/1555 referring to it as St George the Martyr.
- King Henry had a dramatic influence on the way churches were run.
- King Henry owned much of the land between The Highway and the moor.
- Queen Elizabeth made Thomas Williams her Speaker and also sold the house and lands at Stowford to him.
- The Tudors were Welsh.
- King Henry died on 28th January 1547.
- There ARE such things as ghosts...

A SELECTION OF PUBLICATIONS

Of

PAGANUS PUBLISHING

Shudder by A A Prideaux

Who or what is **Shudder**?

The Old Mill was the place in Mill Town where most people worked. Years passed and the mill closed, but something remained inside.

The townspeople had ignored the missing children and the frightening stories of devils and ghosts for as long as they could remember. It was easier to carry on and accept the money the Snooty family provided in return for working at the mill. Everyone allowed the Council members to run their lives and control their ideas without question. Questions were always ignored and the questioner punished. When Lydia Prix returned to the town after her marriage failed, she had no choice but to face the demons of the past and ultimately face the truth. The town would never be the same again.

If you go down to the woods today, you may end up being frightened of more than you think...

The Specials by A A Prideaux is a murder mystery set in 2012.

An old man is found dead in his home and DCI Revie and DS Jackson face the task of discovering who murdered him.

At first, it appears that there is no reason the quiet widower should have been killed. But the investigation soon reveals that the gentle old man had been a long term and particularly deviant paedophile. As the story unfolds throughout the year and the body count rises, the police discover more people who have been living an apparently normal life while successfully hiding their past. The lives of all the people involved can never be the same again. The Specials reaches its dramatic conclusion in Snowdonia.

A Christmas Story by A A Prideaux begins in a modest home in early Edwardian Leeds, where the Prideaux family await a surprise event on Christmas Day 1902. The story takes the reader from 1902 to 1993 in a short story and gives a flavour of what Christmas meant to Clifford and his family. A Christmas Story gives a flavour of the times prior to the Great War for those with no money and no property. What the family had, was their love for each other and that love cannot be exaggerated. A A Prideaux has written about each of her Prideaux ancestors from 1040 to the present day. A Christmas Story is one of her fictionalised tales which draw on known facts. In this case, the story is written with personal experience of the author. This Clifford Prideaux (1902-1963) story takes us to Leeds and a tiny stone cottage full of love and warmth. "*A Christmas Story is about my grandma and grandad. Christmas was always a special time for Grandad Clifford. It's magic ran through his veins from the first day. Clifford was a kind man, but also a mystical one. Even after his death, he has visited his family on many occasions. I think of him as a hermit character, cloaked and walking with a long staff. He appeared in his role of Clifford for only 60 years before he returned to being the hermit.*" **A A Prideaux**.

The story of 'The Bishop and the Witch' by A A Prideaux takes place between 1596 and 1608. John Prideaux was born near Dartmoor in 1578 and eventually became Bishop of Worcester. He spent most of his adult life at Exeter College, Oxford as Regius Professor and Vice Chancellor.

He was involved in many of the important events which took place in England during the reigns of Elizabeth I, James I and Charles I.

When John Prideaux gave evidence in 1606 at the Star Chamber about Anne Gunter, he did so as a well-known and respected Oxford academic.

At the 1604 Witch Trial at Abingdon her alleged tormentors, Elizabeth Gregory, Agnes and Mary Pepwell were ultimately found to be innocent. Anne was sent to stay with Henry Cotton, the Bishop of Salisbury until her father confronted the King and asked him to intervene in the bewitching case.

King James took a personal interest in Anne's troubles and put her under the control of Richard Bancroft, the Archbishop of Canterbury. Anne later confessed to King James that her symptoms were faked on the instructions of her father, Brian Gunter. He was arrested and faced his accusers at the Star Chamber in 1606.

Anne Gunter was given a dowry by King James and she disappeared from the history books. History does not tell us what happened to Anne Gunter, but A A Prideaux provides us with a potential solution. A A Prideaux tells the story of the possible meeting of John Prideaux and Anne Gunter at a much earlier time and how that meeting could have had a bearing on the outcome of the trial. Most of the characters playing a part in this story actually existed, making her version of events a possible one.

"John and Anne become friends and allies and we find that the story was not such a simple one. We discover who the real witches were and how John struggled with his faith during his involvement with the Gunter family. The reader must draw their own conclusions whether the events were caused by demons or drugs. This is an alternative tale based on historical facts and a lot of artistic license."

A A Prideaux

Thank you. Do call again.